SPIRIT

★ of the ★

USA

ACTIVITY BOOK

CLAIRE SAUNDERS

ILLUSTRATED BY THOMAS PATERSON

Kane Miller
A DIVISION OF EDC PUBLISHING

CONTENTS

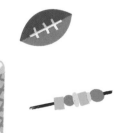

Welcome to the
SPIRIT OF THE USA
ACTIVITY BOOK

Many different things help to make the US the country it is today—foods, customs, people, inventions, celebrations, holidays, sports, folklore, and more. As you color and puzzle your way through this activity book, you'll discover fascinating facts about the history, culture, and spirit of the United States.

First, read the fun facts on these pages, then grab your pens and pencils and dive into the activities!

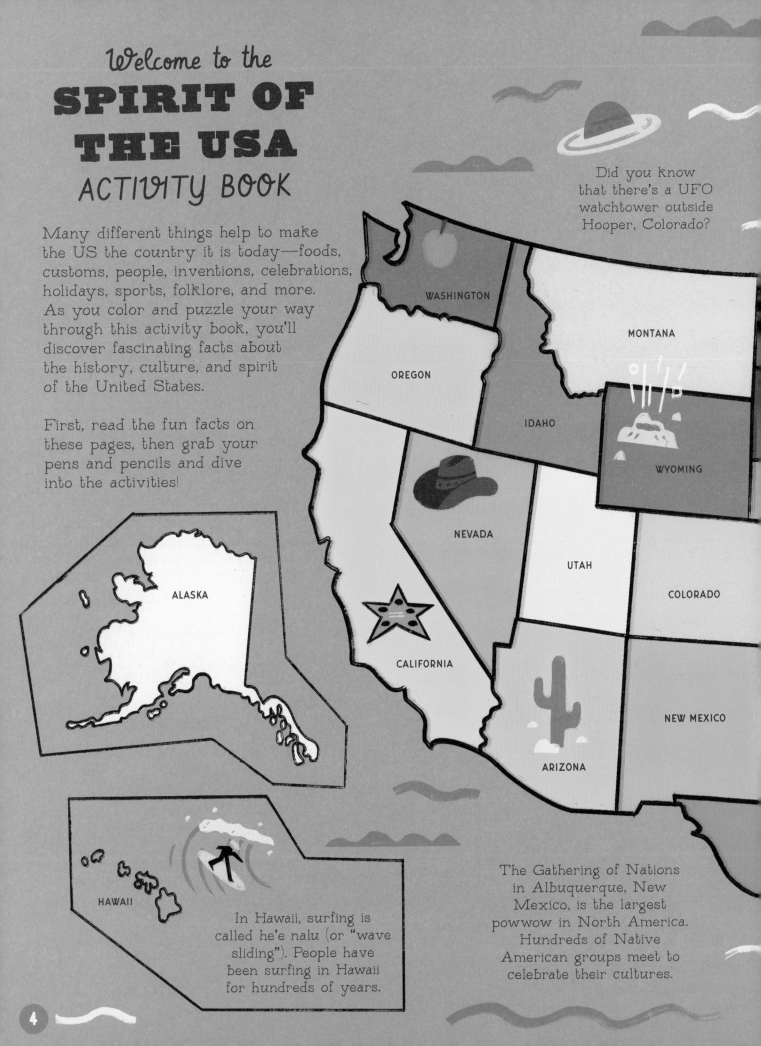

Did you know that there's a UFO watchtower outside Hooper, Colorado?

WASHINGTON

MONTANA

OREGON

IDAHO

WYOMING

NEVADA

UTAH

COLORADO

ALASKA

CALIFORNIA

NEW MEXICO

ARIZONA

HAWAII

In Hawaii, surfing is called he'e nalu (or "wave sliding"). People have been surfing in Hawaii for hundreds of years.

The Gathering of Nations in Albuquerque, New Mexico, is the largest powwow in North America. Hundreds of Native American groups meet to celebrate their cultures.

Halloween lasts for a whole month in Anoka, Minnesota—the "Halloween Capital of the World."

More than half of all US presidents so far were born in just four states: Virginia, Ohio, New York, and Massachusetts.

NORTH DAKOTA

MINNESOTA

SOUTH DAKOTA

WISCONSIN

MICHIGAN

MAINE

VERMONT

NEW HAMPSHIRE

MASSACHUSETTS

NEW YORK

RHODE ISLAND

CONNECTICUT

NEBRASKA

IOWA

ILLINOIS

INDIANA

OHIO

PENNSYLVANIA

NEW JERSEY

DELAWARE

MARYLAND

WEST VIRGINIA

VIRGINIA

KANSAS

MISSOURI

KENTUCKY

NORTH CAROLINA

TENNESSEE

SOUTH CAROLINA

OKLAHOMA

ARKANSAS

MISSISSIPPI

ALABAMA

GEORGIA

TEXAS

LOUISIANA

FLORIDA

Cheerleading used to be an all-male sport. It started at Princeton University, in New Jersey, in the late 19th century.

Florida's eastern coastline is nicknamed the "Space Coast" because of the NASA missions that launch from Kennedy Space Center on Merritt Island.

The city of New Orleans in Louisiana is nicknamed "The Big Easy." This nickname perfectly captures its residents' laid-back lifestyles.

BEFORE *you get* STARTED...

This page shows just some of the foods, festivals, and sports included in this book. How well do you know them?

Check off all of the foods you've tried. Which is your favorite? Circle it.

S'MORES ☐

ICE CREAM SODA ☐

PUMPKIN PIE ☐

CORN DOGS ☐

ALBUQUERQUE BALLOON FIESTA ☐

KENTUCKY DERBY ☐

HOUSTON RODEO ☐

MARDI GRAS ☐

Check the box of any event you have seen, on TV or in real life. Circle the one you would most like to go to.

Have you seen a live game of any of these sports? If so, check the boxes. Then circle the sport you most like to watch or play.

BASKETBALL ☐

ICE HOCKEY ☐

SOCCER ☐

BASEBALL ☐

TRUMPET ☐

DRUM ☐

DOUBLE BASS ☐

SAXOPHONE ☐

Have you heard these instruments being played? Check the boxes of the ones you've heard. Circle the one you would most like to learn to play.

WHERE AM I?

As you go through the puzzles in this book, look for the sights, places, and events pictured below. Once you find them, fill in the name of the state where they can be found or experienced.

BUTTER COW

STATE: _____

ROSWELL UFO SITE

STATE: _____

GOLD NUGGETS

STATE: _____

UNDERWATER MUSIC FESTIVAL

STATE: _____

I-SPY
4TH OF JULY

EVERY YEAR ON THE FOURTH OF JULY, PEOPLE ALL OVER THE US CELEBRATE INDEPENDENCE DAY. THERE ARE PARADES, FIREWORK DISPLAYS, AND COOKOUTS WITH FAMILY AND FRIENDS. THE HOLIDAY MARKS THE DAY IN 1776 WHEN THE UNITED STATES ADOPTED THE DECLARATION OF INDEPENDENCE AND BECAME ITS OWN COUNTRY.

STUDY THIS PICTURE AND FIND:

- 5 ROCKETS
- 4 STRIPED BALLOONS
- 3 BARBECUES
- 2 DRUMS
- 1 US FLAG

Stars & Stripes Puzzle

Flag Day, on June 14th, celebrates the Stars and Stripes—one of America's most important symbols. The flag has 50 stars, one for each state. Its 13 stripes represent the original 13 colonies that gained independence from Great Britain.

This puzzle is missing three of its pieces. Can you work out which of the pieces below will complete it? Circle the three correct pieces.

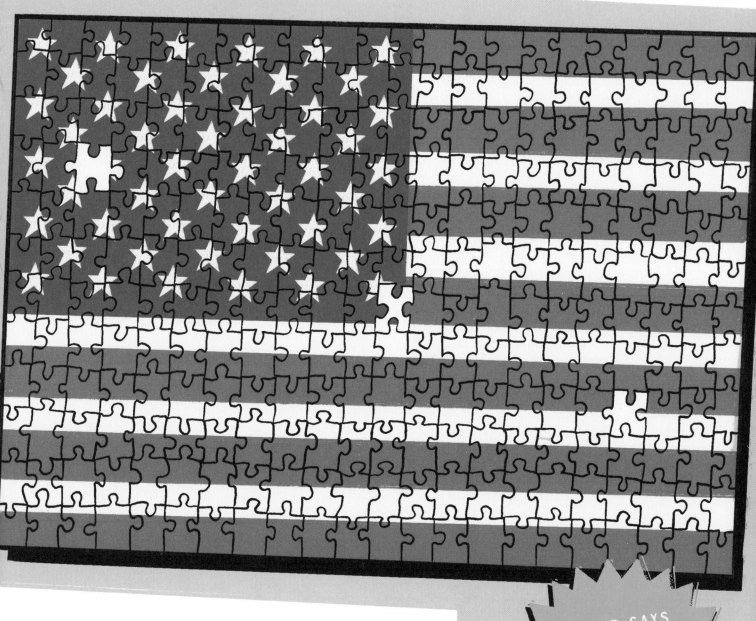

LEGEND SAYS THE VERY FIRST US FLAG WAS SEWN BY A WOMAN NAMED BETSY ROSS IN 1776.

STATE CAPITAL WORD SEARCH

Do you know how your state capital got its name? Many places were named after people—explorers, early settlers, or presidents. Others got their name from local rivers, lakes, or mountains. Some were named after faraway English towns across the ocean.

Find the state capitals in the word search. They can be written forward, backward, up, down, or diagonally. You only need to find the name of the city, not the state.

E	S	Y	T	I	C	E	K	A	L	T	L	A	S
K	E	P	L	R	Y	P	L	I	N	C	O	L	N
D	N	S	R	Q	U	E	K	G	S	K	L	M	G
L	R	E	S	I	B	C	O	L	U	M	B	U	S
I	M	F	H	A	N	N	O	S	K	C	A	J	F
T	C	H	E	E	H	G	R	K	E	V	J	P	U
T	O	P	E	K	A	A	F	B	O	S	T	O	N
L	A	E	U	M	U	E	L	I	T	E	M	R	L
E	T	E	D	N	T	F	S	L	E	L	K	E	Q
R	P	D	O	T	Z	M	D	G	A	L	S	B	G
O	M	F	V	Z	G	D	V	H	P	T	D	K	V
C	R	C	E	Q	F	R	I	C	H	M	O	N	D
K	Y	K	R	X	D	H	A	R	T	F	O	R	D
U	J	E	F	F	E	R	S	O	N	C	I	T	Y

Named after the local landscape:

LITTLE ROCK (ARKANSAS)
SALT LAKE CITY (UTAH)
SPRINGFIELD (ILLINOIS)

Named after people:

JACKSON (MISSISSIPPI)
JEFFERSON CITY (MISSOURI)
LINCOLN (NEBRASKA)
COLUMBUS (OHIO)

Indigenous American names:

TALLAHASSEE (FLORIDA)
TOPEKA (KANSAS)

Named after towns in England:

DOVER (DELAWARE)
BOSTON (MASSACHUSETTS)
HARTFORD (CONNECTICUT)
RICHMOND (VIRGINIA)

BEFORE ST. PAUL, MINNESOTA, GOT ITS NAME IN 1849, IT WAS CALLED PIG'S EYE!

PAUL BUNYAN WAS A GIANT

WHO COULD EAT 50

IN A MINUTE. HIS SIDEKICK WAS A HUGE BLUE

CALLED BABE.

SAY HELLO TO SOME FAMOUS FOLK HEROES OF THE UNITED STATES. SOME OF THESE PEOPLE WERE INVENTED BY STORYTELLERS. OTHERS WERE REAL PEOPLE, ALTHOUGH THE WILD STORIES TOLD ABOUT THEM WERE OFTEN EXAGGERATED! PEOPLE LOVED TO HEAR "TALL TALES" ABOUT LARGER-THAN-LIFE HEROES.

USE THE WORD BANK TO FILL IN THE MISSING WORDS AND COMPLETE THE TALL TALES. CROSS OFF EACH WORD AS YOU USE IT.

SALLY ANN THUNDER ANN WHIRLWIND CROCKETT MADE A LASSO OUT OF SIX

AND WORE A

AS A BONNET.

MOLLY PITCHER WAS THE NICKNAME GIVEN TO A HEROINE SAID TO HAVE FOUGHT IN THE REVOLUTIONARY WAR. ACCORDING TO THE STORY, A

SHOT STRAIGHT BETWEEN HER LEGS IN THE MIDDLE OF A BATTLE!

MANY TALL TALES WERE TOLD ABOUT DAVY CROCKETT, A REAL-LIFE FRONTIERSMAN AND SOLDIER. ACCORDING TO ONE, HE KILLED A

WHEN HE WAS THREE YEARS OLD.

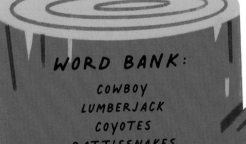

WORD BANK:

COWBOY
LUMBERJACK
COYOTES
RATTLESNAKES
PANCAKES
CANNONBALL
BEAR
OX
HORNET'S NEST
TORNADO

PECOS BILL WAS RAISED IN THE WILD BY

HE GREW UP TO BECOME A

IN THE WILD WEST, WHERE HE FOUGHT OUTLAWS AND LASSOED A

KALEIDOSCOPE of CULTURE

Over 350 different languages are spoken in the US. People from all over the world have come to live here, creating a kaleidoscope of different languages, cultures, races, and religions.

G
S   P   ~~I~~
E   S   H   I
~~S~~   I   N   E
A
N   ~~E~~
H   ~~H~~   ~~C~~   S
L   ~~N~~

Rearrange the letters to make the names of the top-three most-spoken languages in the US. Each letter can only be used once. Some of the letters have been filled in for you.

1. ..... N G .... H

2. S .... N I ....

3. C .... N .... E

Aloha!

THE STATE OF HAWAII HAS ITS OWN LANGUAGE, AND ITS OWN ALPHABET. THIS IS MADE UP OF 12 LETTERS AND THE 'OKINA, WHICH SOUNDS LIKE THE BREAK IN THE MIDDLE OF THE WORD "UH-OH" AND IS WRITTEN USING A ' SYMBOL. HAWAIIAN ALSO USES DIPHTHONGS, WHICH ARE PAIRS OF VOWELS THAT MAKE A NEW SOUND.

HOW MANY WORDS CAN YOU MAKE USING ONLY THE LETTERS IN THE HAWAIIAN ALPHABET? ALL WORDS MUST BE THREE OR MORE LETTERS.

A, E, H, I, K, L, M, N, O, P, U, W

POW LIME HIKE
nope

HOW DID YOU DO?

- UP TO 15 WORDS: GOOD EFFORT

- 16–29 WORDS: EXCELLENT

- 30+ WORDS: OUTSTANDING!

WHAT'S WRONG ON THE TRAIL?

IN THE MIDDLE OF THE 19TH CENTURY, LARGE GROUPS OF SETTLERS HEADED ALONG THE OREGON TRAIL IN SEARCH OF A BETTER LIFE IN THE WEST. THE JOURNEY FROM MISSOURI TO OREGON TOOK AROUND FIVE MONTHS. MANY FAMILIES HAD TO FIT ALL OF THEIR BELONGINGS, AS WELL AS FOOD FOR THE JOURNEY, INTO ONE SMALL WAGON!

TAKE A LOOK AT THIS PICTURE OF THE OREGON TRAIL. CAN YOU SPOT SIX THINGS THAT DON'T BELONG?

GOLD RUSH!

What's that glinting in the stream? Eureka! It's a shiny gold nugget! Hundreds of thousands of people flooded to California in the middle of the 19th century hoping to strike gold and make their fortune.

Imagine you are a hopeful fortune hunter panning for gold. Can you work out where the nugget is hidden in the grid? Follow the instructions, using the compass to help you. When you find the nugget, mark the location with an X.

- Start in the southeast corner
- Move 4 squares west
- Move 2 squares northeast
- Move 3 squares north
- Move 2 squares west
- Move 4 squares southeast

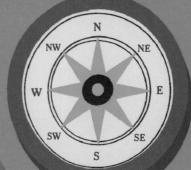

RODEO RECALL

RODEO IS THE OFFICIAL STATE SPORT OF THREE STATES: SOUTH DAKOTA, WYOMING, AND TEXAS. AT THE HOUSTON RODEO, IN TEXAS, DARING COWBOYS AND COWGIRLS PUT THEIR SKILL AND SPEED TO THE TEST IN EVENTS SUCH AS BARREL RACING, ROPING CALVES, AND BRONC RIDING (RIDING A BUCKING HORSE).

STUDY THE PICTURE BELOW FOR 1 MINUTE. THEN COVER IT UP AND ANSWER THE QUESTIONS AT THE BOTTOM OF THE PAGE. DON'T PEEK AT THE QUESTIONS FIRST!

1. What color is the horse's mane? ....

2. How many American flags are there in the picture? ....

3. What number is written on the barrel? ....

4. What color are the cowboy's boots? ....

ALIEN IN AMERICA

The most famous UFO (unidentified flying object) in history crash-landed near Roswell, New Mexico, in 1947—or so some people believed! In fact, the mysterious wreckage wasn't an alien spacecraft at all, but a top secret spy balloon launched by the US military.

Imagine you are an alien who has crash-landed in the US. Write a postcard to your home planet, telling your friends all about the US. What do you like best about it?

Off TO THE FAIR

The Iowa State Fair is one of the biggest state fairs in the US. It's been running for over 160 years! Test your smarts with these multiple-choice questions. Circle the correct answers.

1. Every year, the fair exhibits a butter cow—a life-size sculpture made from (you guessed it!) butter. The sculpture is big enough to butter how many slices of toast?

A) 192   B) 1,920   C) 19,200

2. Which of these contests is NOT an annual event at the fair?

A) COW CHIP THROWING   B) IGLOO BUILDING
C) HOG CALLING

3. The winner of 2012's Big Boar competition was a hog called Reggie who weighed a record-breaking 1,335 pounds. This is about the same as how many bricks?

A) 30   B) 300   C) 3,000

4. The fair is famous for a certain kind of food. What is it?

A) FOOD ON A STICK   B) FRIED FLIES
C) A $1,000 HOT DOG

5. Which of these presidents has never visited the fair?

A) DWIGHT EISENHOWER   B) BARACK OBAMA
C) THOMAS JEFFERSON

UP, UP, AND AWAY!

LOOK AT THIS SKY FILLED WITH BALLOONS! THE ALBUQUERQUE BALLOON FIESTA, HELD IN NEW MEXICO EVERY FALL, IS THE WORLD'S LARGEST HOT-AIR BALLOON FESTIVAL.

BY MOVING FROM BALLOON TO BALLOON, CAN YOU FIND A ROUTE FROM THE GROUND UP TO THE CLOUDS? YOU CAN ONLY USE THE ODD-NUMBERED BALLOONS.

END

37

88

90

24

86

73

21

49

44

17

76

81

72

55

26

74

69

72

23

21

21

98

34

75

74

19

74

43

51

33

12

54

87

99

91

86

22

66

35

79

44

73

6

21

21

21

9

START

THE FIRST AMERICANS

LONG BEFORE EUROPEAN SETTLERS ARRIVED, NORTH AMERICA WAS HOME TO INDIGENOUS AMERICANS. THERE ARE MORE THAN 570 INDIGENOUS AMERICAN NATIONS IN THE UNITED STATES TODAY, EACH WITH THEIR OWN CULTURE.

FILL IN THE CRISSCROSS GRID WITH THE NAMES OF THE INDIGENOUS NATIONS BELOW.

9 LETTERS
BLACKFEET
CHICKASAW

8 LETTERS
CHEROKEE
CHIPPEWA
KOOTENAI

7 LETTERS
CHOCTAW

CHICKASAW

DID YOU KNOW THAT THE NAMES OF OVER HALF THE STATES IN THE US COME FROM INDIGENOUS AMERICAN LANGUAGES?

6 LETTERS
NAVAJO
APACHE
PUEBLO
LUMBEE

5 LETTERS
SIOUX
CREEK

PATTERN MATCH

The Navajo, an Indigenous tribe from the Southwest, are known for their amazing weaving skills. Their blankets and rugs are often covered with zigzags, stripes, and diamond patterns in a variety of colors, including red, green, gold, and blue.

One half of a rug has been drawn in the space below. Complete the picture by drawing the other, identical half, then color it in.

SOCCER JERSEY TRIANGLE

The US women's national soccer team is one of the best in the world. They've won several World Cups and Olympic gold medals.

These soccer jerseys are missing their numbers, from 1 to 6. Write the numbers on the jerseys, so that the numbers on each side of the triangle add up to 9. One of the numbers has been added for you.

CRACK THE SUPER BOWL CODES

More Americans watch football than any other sport. Every year, the two winning teams from the National Football League (NFL) season play each other at the championship Super Bowl game. Millions of fans meet up with friends and family to watch the big game.

Crack the codes to discover some fun facts about Super Bowl Sunday. Use the tables to help you. First find the coded letter on the top row of the table—the letter below it is the answer.

1. THE LETTERS IN THIS CODE HAVE BEEN SHIFTED ONE TO THE RIGHT.

A	B	C	D	E	F	G	H	I	J	K	L	M	N	O	P	Q	R	S	T	U	V	W	X	Y	Z
B	C	D	E	F	G	H	I	J	K	L	M	N	O	P	Q	R	S	T	U	V	W	X	Y	Z	A

WHICH TEAM, FROM MASSACHUSETTS, HAS PLAYED IN THE MOST SUPER BOWLS?

M D V   D M F K Z M C   O Z S Q H N S R

2. THE LETTERS IN THIS CODE HAVE BEEN SHIFTED ONE TO THE LEFT.

A	B	C	D	E	F	G	H	I	J	K	L	M	N	O	P	Q	R	S	T	U	V	W	X	Y	Z
Z	A	B	C	D	E	F	G	H	I	J	K	L	M	N	O	P	Q	R	S	T	U	V	W	X	Y

WHICH PLAYER HAS WON THE MOST SUPER BOWL CHAMPIONSHIPS?

U P N   C S B E Z

3. ALL THE LETTERS IN THIS CODE HAVE BEEN SHIFTED EITHER ONE TO THE RIGHT OR ONE TO THE LEFT. USE THE TWO TABLES ABOVE TO WORK OUT WHICH LETTERS ARE THE CORRECT ONES.

AROUND 12.5 MILLION OF THESE ARE EATEN IN THE US EVERY SUPER BOWL SUNDAY—WHAT ARE THEY?

O   J   A  A   B   T

□OR□   □OR□   □OR□   □OR□   □OR□   □OR□

□□□□□□

BASEBALL
MATCHUP

BASEBALL HAS BEEN POPULAR IN THE US SINCE THE 1840S. THAT'S WHY IT'S CALLED "AMERICA'S FAVORITE PASTIME." 30 TEAMS (29 IN THE US, ONE IN CANADA) PLAY IN MAJOR LEAGUE BASEBALL (MLB).

CAN YOU MATCH THESE BASEBALL TEAMS TO THEIR HOME CITIES? DRAW LINES TO CONNECT EACH PAIR. TO HELP YOU, EACH TEAM NAME ALSO HAS A PICTURE OF A FAMOUS LANDMARK FROM THEIR CITY.

YANKEES

Cardinals

NATIONALS

RED SOX

GIANTS

ST. LOUIS
(MISSOURI)

WASHINGTON,
D.C.

SAN FRANCISCO
(CALIFORNIA)

NEW YORK CITY
(NEW YORK)

BOSTON
(MASSACHUSETTS)

BASKETBALL BRAINTEASER

BASKETBALL WAS INVENTED IN SPRINGFIELD, MASSACHUSETTS, IN 1891. THE ORIGINAL HOOPS WERE MADE FROM PEACH BASKETS!

TAKE A LOOK AT THIS MATCHSTICK PUZZLE BELOW. CAN YOU MOVE TWO MATCHSTICKS SO THAT THE BASKETBALL ENDS UP OUTSIDE THE MATCHSTICK HOOP? YOU CAN MOVE THEM HOWEVER YOU LIKE, AS LONG AS THE HOOP REMAINS THE SAME SHAPE IT STARTED IN.

IT'S A GOAL!

DID YOU KNOW THAT THE FIRST HOCKEY PUCKS WERE MADE FROM FROZEN COW POOP?

WHOOSH! ICE HOCKEY IS ONE OF THE SPEEDIEST SPORTS. PLAYERS STRIKE RUBBER DISKS CALLED PUCKS ACROSS THE ICE AT SPEEDS OF UP TO 100 MILES PER HOUR!

FOLLOW THE LINES TO FIND OUT WHICH PLAYER ZIPS ACROSS THE ICE AND SCORES A GOAL.

A

B

C

THE GOAL SCORER IS PLAYER:

_____

Derby Draw

The Kentucky Derby is a famous horse race held every May in Louisville, Kentucky. The 1.25-mile race is all over in around two minutes! It's known as "The Most Exciting Two Minutes in Sports."

Color in this scene. Each jockey's jersey needs to be a different pattern—you could use stripes, spots, or diamonds. Then make up some names for the horses. They can be as silly as you like—previous winners have been called Super Saver, Spend a Buck, and Behave Yourself.

Name:

Name:

Name:

MOTOR
RACE MATCH

IT'S RACE DAY IN SPEEDWAY, INDIANA! THE INDIANAPOLIS 500, ALSO KNOWN AS THE INDY 500, IS ONE OF THE MOST FAMOUS MOTOR RACES IN THE WORLD. THE 500-MILE RACE TAKES PLACE EVERY MAY AT THE HUGE INDIANAPOLIS MOTOR SPEEDWAY.

DRAW LINES TO CONNECT THE FOUR DRIVERS TO THE CARS OF THE SAME COLOR.

RULES:

- ONLY 1 LINE IN EACH SQUARE
- THE LINES CAN GO UP AND DOWN, LEFT AND RIGHT, BUT NOT DIAGONALLY
- THE LINES MUST NOT CROSS

EXAMPLE:

AN INDY 500 TRADITION IS THAT THE WINNER OF THE RACE IS GIVEN MILK TO DRINK.

THE ZOOPOLIS 500 RACE IS HELD AT THE SAME TIME AS THE INDY 500, AT THE INDIANAPOLIS ZOO. THE COMPETITORS ARE TORTOISES!

Presidents Crossword

Read the clues and fill in the crossword with the names of ten famous American presidents. Use the word bank at the bottom of the page to help you. You only need to write the presidents' last names, not their first names.

ACROSS:

2 The youngest person ever elected president (7)

5 The country's first African American president (5)

6 First president of the United States (10)

9 President who also drafted the Declaration of Independence (9)

10 President during World War I (6)

DOWN:

1 This president's face features on the front of the $50 bill (5)

3 This president created the interstate highway system (10)

4 President after whom the teddy bear was named (9)

7 President who ended slavery and led the nation through the Civil War (7)

8 President at the end of World War II (6)

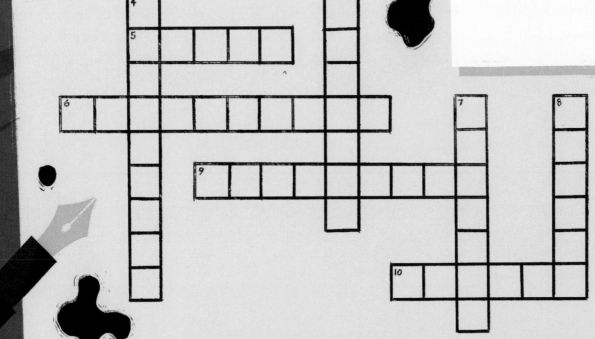

WORD BANK

George Washington, Thomas Jefferson, Abraham Lincoln, Ulysses S. Grant, Theodore Roosevelt, Woodrow Wilson, Harry S. Truman, Dwight Eisenhower, John F. Kennedy, Barack Obama.

WHO AM I?

Throughout American history, some groups of people have had to fight for their civil rights. These are the basic rights of every person to be treated equally and fairly, regardless of their race, gender, or other factors.

Read these descriptions of American civil rights heroes, then draw a line to match each description with the correct name.

MARTIN LUTHER KING JR.

HARRIET TUBMAN

HELEN KELLER

SUSAN B. ANTHONY

ROSA PARKS

I was a leader of the American Civil Rights Movement. In 1963, I gave a famous speech, "I Have a Dream."

I ESCAPED FROM SLAVERY IN 1849 USING THE UNDERGROUND RAILROAD. LATER, I RISKED MY LIFE HELPING MANY OTHERS TO ESCAPE.

I FOUGHT AGAINST RACIAL SEGREGATION. IN 1955 IN MONTGOMERY, ALABAMA, I REFUSED TO GIVE UP MY SEAT ON A BUS TO A WHITE PERSON.

I WAS BLIND AND DEAF, BUT LEARNED HOW TO READ AND TALK. I SPENT MY LIFE RAISING AWARENESS FOR PEOPLE WITH DISABILITIES.

In the 19th century, I campaigned to help American women win the right to vote.

JAZZ SUDOKU

HAVE YOU EVER LISTENED TO A TYPE OF
MUSIC CALLED JAZZ? THE VERY FIRST
JAZZ MUSIC CAME FROM THE US. JAZZ
BEGAN IN AFRICAN AMERICAN COMMUNITIES
IN NEW ORLEANS, LOUISIANA.

COMPLETE THE SUDOKU PUZZLE BY FILLING EACH
SQUARE WITH A PICTURE OF A TRUMPET,
A DRUM, A SAXOPHONE, OR A DOUBLE BASS.
EACH ROW, COLUMN, AND MINI GRID MUST CONTAIN
ALL FOUR OF THE JAZZ BAND INSTRUMENTS.

MARDI GRAS
MEMORY CHALLENGE

MARDI GRAS IS A CARNIVAL. IT TAKES PLACE THROUGHOUT THE FIRST FEW MONTHS OF THE YEAR. NEW ORLEANS, LOUISIANA, HOSTS ONE OF THE BIGGEST MARDI GRAS PARTIES IN THE WORLD. PEOPLE DRESS UP IN COSTUMES, DANCE AT MASKED BALLS, AND LINE THE STREETS TO WATCH PARADES OF MARCHING BANDS AND FLOATS. PEOPLE ON THE FLOATS THROW BEADS, TRINKETS, AND TOY COINS CALLED DOUBLOONS INTO THE CROWD.

PICTURED BELOW AND RIGHT ARE EIGHT OBJECTS YOU MIGHT SEE AT MARDI GRAS. STUDY THE PICTURE FOR 1 MINUTE, THEN COVER IT WITH A PIECE OF PAPER, AND WRITE DOWN AS MANY OF THE EIGHT ITEMS AS YOU CAN REMEMBER.

1. _____

2. _____

3. _____

4. _____

5. _____

6. _____

7. _____

8. _____

Music City

ROCK, POP, HIP HOP, JAZZ, COUNTRY—WHATEVER TYPE OF MUSIC YOU LIKE TO LISTEN TO, YOU CAN FIND SOMEONE PLAYING IT IN NASHVILLE, TENNESSEE. THE CITY IS EVEN KNOWN AS "MUSIC CITY."

IMAGINE YOU ARE IN A BAND WITH YOUR FRIENDS. THINK UP A NAME AND LOGO FOR YOUR BAND, AND DRAW IT ON THE DRUM KIT BELOW. THEN WRITE DOWN THE NAMES OF WHO PLAYS EACH INSTRUMENT.

SINGER:

GUITAR:

DRUMS:

KEYBOARD:

Made in the USA

TAKE A LOOK AT THE YUMMY FOODS BELOW. THEY WERE ALL INVENTED IN THE UNITED STATES! IN EACH ROW, CIRCLE THE ONE PICTURE THAT'S DIFFERENT FROM THE REST.

THE ICE CREAM SODA WAS INVENTED IN THE 1860S OR 1870S, THOUGH NO ONE QUITE KNOWS WHERE. SODA MAKERS IN PHILADELPHIA (PENNSYLVANIA), DETROIT (MICHIGAN), AND ELIZABETH (NEW JERSEY) ALL CLAIMED CREDIT FOR THE IDEA!

SWEET TEA WAS INVENTED IN SOUTH CAROLINA IN THE LATE 19TH CENTURY.

THE FIRST CHOCOLATE CHIP COOKIES WERE BAKED BY RUTH WAKEFIELD IN MASSACHUSETTS IN 1930.

THE RECIPE FOR S'MORES FIRST APPEARED IN A GIRL SCOUTS' GUIDEBOOK IN 1927.

CORN DOGS—BATTERED, DEEP-FRIED HOT DOGS ON STICK—WERE INVENTED F THE 1942 TEXAS STATE FA

A SLICE of PIE

Have you ever heard the phrase "as American as apple pie"? The dessert is a much-loved symbol of America.

Can you split this delicious apple pie into seven pieces, using just three cuts?

Apple pie is the state pie of Vermont. Other states with fruity state pies include Maine (blueberry pie), Delaware (peach pie), Florida (key lime pie), and Illinois (pumpkin pie—yes, pumpkin is a fruit!).

What's for BREAKFAST?

WHETHER IT'S BREAKFAST BURRITOS IN NEW MEXICO, BISCUITS AND GRAVY IN WEST VIRGINIA, OR STACKS OF FLUFFY PANCAKES SMOTHERED IN VERMONT MAPLE SYRUP, AMERICAN BREAKFASTS ARE HARD TO BEAT!

STUDY THE THREE DINER RECEIPTS BELOW, THEN WORK OUT THE COST OF EACH ITEM AND FILL IN THE MISSING PRICES ON THE MENU.

BREAKFAST Menu

ORANGE JUICE $ _____

STACK OF PANCAKES $ _____

BLUEBERRIES $ _____

3 × orange juices

= $9

2 × orange juices
1 × stack of pancakes

= $12

1 × stack of pancakes
1 × blueberries

= $8

ON THE ROAD

The summer road trip is a classic all-American experience. Let's hit the road and take a trip around the US, visiting some of the country's weird and wonderful roadside attractions!

Your road trip starts and ends in Florida. The instructions below will guide you around the map. If you follow them correctly, your route will take you past five attractions. Check them off the list as you pass them.

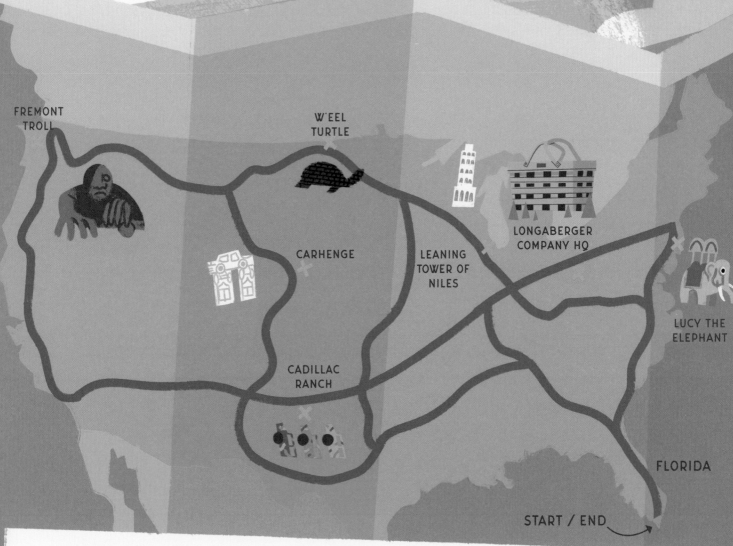

FREMONT TROLL

W'EEL TURTLE

CARHENGE

LEANING TOWER OF NILES

LONGABERGER COMPANY HQ

LUCY THE ELEPHANT

CADILLAC RANCH

FLORIDA

START / END

INSTRUCTIONS:

• If you arrive at a fork in the path, always head left.

• At a crossroads, go straight ahead.

Fremont Troll—under a bridge in Seattle, Washington ☐

W'eel Turtle—Dunseith, North Dakota ☐

Leaning Tower of Niles—Niles, Illinois ☐

Longaberger Company HQ—Newark, Ohio ☐

Lucy the Elephant—Margate, New Jersey ☐

Carhenge—Alliance, Nebraska ☐

Cadillac Ranch—Amarillo, Texas ☐

WHICH STATES on the Plates?

On a road trip, it's fun to spot license plates from different states. Can you unscramble the letters on these made-up license plates to work out which state each one is from?

MALOHAKO
IGE - 901
THE SOONER STATE

_ _ _ _ _ _ _ _

VADANE
248 · UGM
The Silver State

_ _ _ _ _ _

AIHIWA
MNG - 728
ALOHA STATE

_ _ _ _ _ _

ROHED SADLIN
VO - 820
Ocean State

_ _ _ _ _

_ _ _ _ _ _

Draw a new license plate design for your home state. Include the name of the state and make up a new nickname for it.

DRIVE-IN

Movie Night

Did you know the drive-in movie was invented in the US? The first real drive-in theater opened in Camden, New Jersey, in 1933.

Look at this picture of a drive-in theater. The car alarm in one of the vehicles has gone off, right in the middle of the movie. How annoying! Can you find the car, using the clues below? Cross out the cars as you eliminate them, then circle the one noisy car that remains.

CLUES:

1. The car isn't red.
2. The car is not in the front row.
3. The car does not have a roof rack.
4. There is more than one person in the car.
5. The car does not have circular taillights.

Oscars Dress-up

Roll out the red carpet! Every year in February or March, movie stars gather in Los Angeles, California, for the world-famous Academy Awards ceremony. Golden statuettes called Oscars are given to the best actress, actor, film director, and other winners.

Draw some clothes onto this award statue. It could be something a Hollywood star might wear to the ceremony. Or it could just be your own favorite outfit!

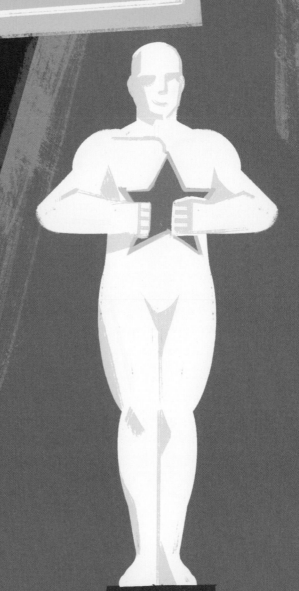

Hollywood Star

Top movie and entertainment stars are honored on the Hollywood Walk of Fame—over 2,500 coral-pink stars set into the sidewalk in Hollywood, California. Each star bears the person's name and a symbol to show what the person is famous for: movies, TV, theater, music, or radio.

Imagine you have a star on the Hollywood Walk of Fame! Write your name on the star, then choose one of the five symbols and draw it below your name, in the circle. At the bottom of the page, write what you have done to deserve your star— for example, you might be a famous musician, a movie star, a talented animator, a costume designer for the theater, or a comedian on TV.

I am famous for...

be a pop
ARTIST

Andy Warhol was a famous American artist who was part of the pop art movement. He liked to make colorful art inspired by popular culture, such as movie stars and advertisements. One of his most famous artworks is 32 pictures of soup cans in different flavors.

Choose an everyday object and draw it in one of the spaces below. It can be anything you like—a sneaker, a tube of toothpaste, or even a can of soup! Copy the image into the other three spaces, then color all four images, using different colors each time.

Give each of the four pictures a different bright-colored background.

ON THE
BOOKSHELF

Books by American authors have delighted readers around the world for centuries. Many have been described as "The Great American Novel," including *The Great Gatsby* by F. Scott Fitzgerald and *To Kill a Mockingbird* by Harper Lee.

Imagine you are an author. Draw the cover for your latest book below. Remember to include the title, and your name. Add a made-up quote from a newspaper or a famous person saying how much they enjoyed your book!

Write the first sentence of your book here. Make it as exciting as possible, so the reader will want to know what happens next!

All the brilliant inventions (and inventors) on this page came from the United States. The timeline shows the year that each one was invented.

There are three blank spaces in the timeline, and three inventions at the top of the page. Can you guess where each invention belongs? Write or draw them on the timeline in the correct position.

Super Soaker
(Lonnie Johnson)

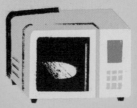

Microwave oven
(Percy Spencer)

Toilet paper
(Joseph Gayetty)

1752
Lightning rod
(Benjamin Franklin)

1857

1893
Ferris wheel
(George Washington Gale Ferris Jr.)

1903
First plane
(Wright brothers)

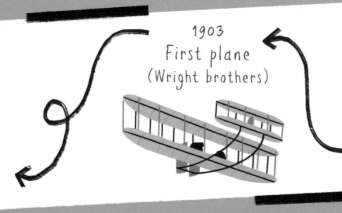

1903
Windshield wipers
(Mary Anderson)

1945

1954
UNIMATE, the first robot
(George Devol)

1966
Home security system
(Marie Van Brittan Brown)

1989

THE GREAT OUTDOORS

THE WORLD'S VERY FIRST NATIONAL PARK, YELLOWSTONE, WAS CREATED IN 1872. TODAY THERE ARE 63 NATIONAL PARKS AROUND THE COUNTRY. MILLIONS OF PEOPLE VISIT THEM EVERY YEAR TO HIKE, CAMP, AND SPEND TIME OUTDOORS.

USE YOUR POWERS OF LOGIC TO WORK OUT WHICH NATIONAL PARK THESE THREE CHILDREN VISITED, AND WHAT THEY DID THERE. READ THE CLUES BELOW, AND FILL IN THE GRID: ADD A CHECK MARK IF YOU FIGURE OUT SOMETHING IS TRUE, AND AN X IF SOMETHING IS FALSE.

	BISCAYNE NATIONAL PARK, FLORIDA	GLACIER NATIONAL PARK, MONTANA	ROCKY MOUNTAIN NATIONAL PARK, COLORADO	HIKING	SNORKELING	WHITE WATER RAFTING
ANTHONY						
AVA						
CHLOE						

CHILD

PLACE · ACTIVITY

CLUES:

1. THE CHILD WHO WENT SNORKELING WAS NOT A GIRL.

2. CHLOE VISITED GLACIER NATIONAL PARK, BUT DID NOT GO HIKING.

3. THE CHILD WHO WENT TO ROCKY MOUNTAIN NATIONAL PARK DID NOT SPEND ANY TIME NEAR WATER.

BIGFOOT
CAMPFIRE STORY

TELLING STORIES AROUND A CAMPFIRE IS A MUCH-LOVED AMERICAN TRADITION. USE YOUR STORYTELLING SKILLS TO FINISH OFF THIS CAMPFIRE TALE ABOUT BIGFOOT. IN AMERICAN FOLKLORE, BIGFOOT (ALSO KNOWN AS SASQUATCH) IS A MYSTERIOUS APELIKE CREATURE WHICH LIVES IN THE FORESTS OF THE NORTHWESTERN US AND CANADA.

BEFORE YOU READ THE STORY, FILL IN THESE WORDS. MAKE THEM AS SILLY AS YOU LIKE!

1. Something tall

2. A color

3. Something smelly

4. Something big

5. A person (someone you know or someone famous)

6. A piece of cutlery

7. Something long and pointy

8. A part of the body

NEXT, ADD THE WORDS INTO THE STORY. THE NUMBERS BY THE SPACES SHOW YOU WHICH WORD TO USE.

It was a dark night. We were camping in the wilderness, when suddenly a terrifying creature appeared. It was as tall as _____ [1], with shaggy _____ [2] fur that smelled of _____ [3]. Each of its footprints was so big, it could fit a whole _____ [4] inside it. In one huge paw it held _____ [5], and in the other a giant _____ [6]! Help! It was Bigfoot and it looked really hungry! Quickly, I grabbed a nearby _____ [7], and used it to tickle Bigfoot's hairy _____ [8]. Bigfoot squealed, dropped _____ [5], and ran away into the trees. Phew!

STATE MOTTO CIPHER

MANY OF THE 50 STATES HAVE THEIR OWN OFFICIAL OR UNOFFICIAL MOTTO. THESE WORDS AND PHRASES WERE CHOSEN BECAUSE THEY REPRESENT THE SPIRIT OF THAT STATE. STATE MOTTOS COME IN MANY LANGUAGES, INCLUDING LATIN, ENGLISH, SPANISH, FRENCH, AND ANCIENT GREEK.

THE CODE BELOW IS CALLED THE PIGPEN CIPHER. EACH LETTER HAS ITS OWN SYMBOL THAT MATCHES THE PART OF THE GRID IT IS IN—FOR EXAMPLE, ⌐ IS THE LETTER A, ⌐ IS THE LETTER J, AND ⌄ IS THE LETTER S. USE THE CIPHER TO CRACK THE CODES BELOW, REVEALING THE STATE TO WHICH EACH MOTTO BELONGS.

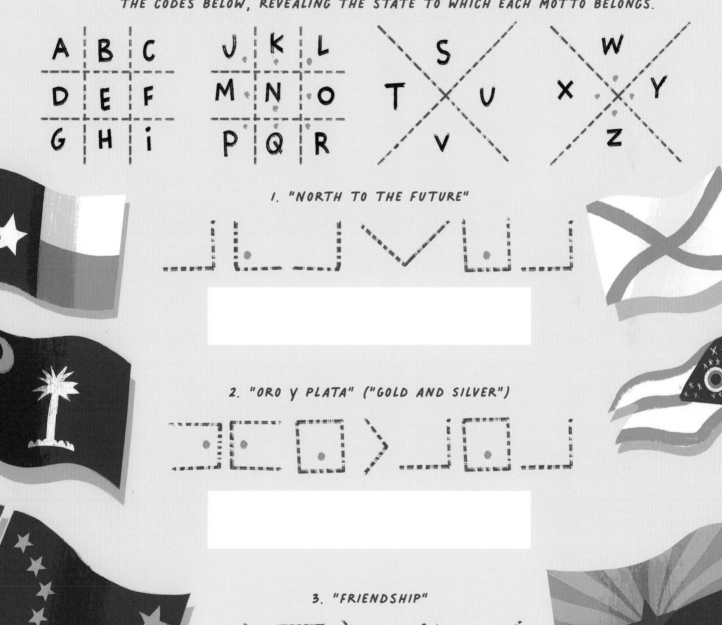

1. "NORTH TO THE FUTURE"

2. "ORO Y PLATA" ("GOLD AND SILVER")

3. "FRIENDSHIP"

Funny Festivals

Hundreds of festivals take place all over the US—including the fabulous events on this page! Pick the one you'd most like to go to, and design a poster for it.

Potato Days—Clark, South Dakota

A celebration of the potato, with a "Best Decorated Potato" competition and a "Mashed Potato Wrestling" contest.

Underwater Music Festival—Florida Keys

An underwater concert played by mermaids and musician-divers.

BugFest—Raleigh, North Carolina

Play bug games, meet bug scientists, and eat bug dishes made from insects!

Draw a
BALD EAGLE

The bald eagle was chosen as the national emblem of the United States in 1782. The bird appears on the Great Seal, and on many coins. It was also chosen for the mission patch of Apollo 11—the spaceflight that first landed humans on the moon.

Follow these simple steps to draw a bald eagle in the space below, then color it in.

1

2

3

4

BOSTON MARATHON MAZE

THE BOSTON MARATHON IS A FAMOUS 26-MILE RACE WHICH IS HELD EVERY APRIL IN GREATER BOSTON, MASSACHUSETTS. IT WAS FIRST RUN IN 1897, MAKING IT THE WORLD'S OLDEST ANNUAL MARATHON.

RACE THROUGH THIS MAZE FROM THE STARTING POINT TO THE FINISH LINE. YOU WILL NEED TO PASS THE FOUR BOSTON LANDMARKS ALONG THE MARATHON ROUTE IN THE ORDER THEY ARE LISTED. READY, SET, **GO!**

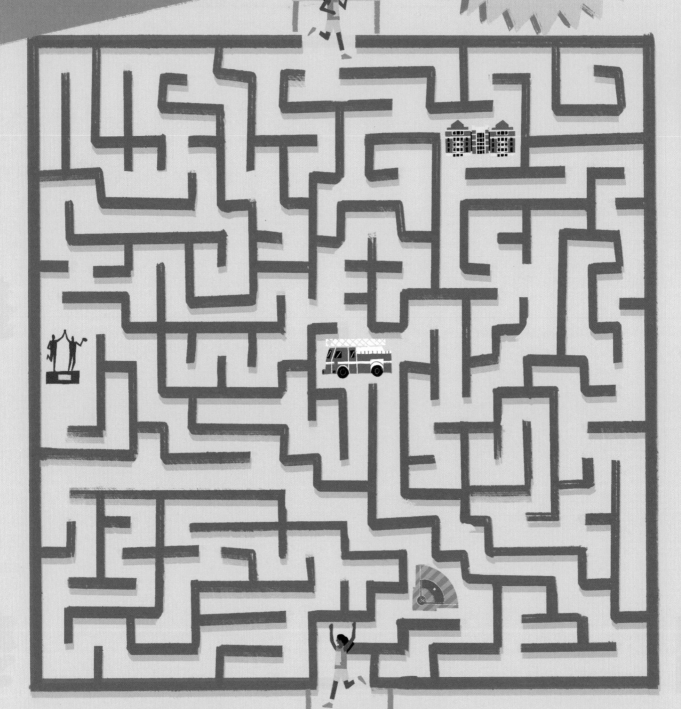

LANDMARKS

 1. WELLESLEY COLLEGE

 2. NEWTON FIRE STATION

 3. JOHNNY KELLEY STATUE

 4. FENWAY PARK BASEBALL PARK

Which Food, WHICH STATE?

SOME STATES ARE KNOWN FOR CERTAIN FOODS. EACH OF THE FOODS ON THIS PAGE HAS A LABEL, WHICH SHOWS THE TWO-LETTER ABBREVIATION OF THE STATE THE FOOD COMES FROM. DRAW A LINE FROM EACH FOOD TO THE MATCHING STATE NAME AT THE BOTTOM OF THE PAGE.

POTATOES
ID

BLUE CRAB
MD

HAM
VA

LOBSTER
ME

PEACHES
GA

WILD SALMON
AK

CORN
IA

CHEDDAR CHEESE
WI

WISCONSIN

ALASKA

IOWA

MARYLAND

MAINE

GEORGIA

IDAHO

VIRGINIA

HAPPY HALLOWEEN!

OCTOBER 31ST IS HALLOWEEN! CHILDREN DRESS UP IN SPOOKY OR FUN COSTUMES AND KNOCK ON NEIGHBORHOOD DOORS, CALLING "TRICK OR TREAT!" AND COLLECTING CANDY.

DRAW SOME HALLOWEEN DECORATIONS ON THIS HOUSE, THEN COLOR IT IN.

IDEAS:

- DRAW JACK-O'-LANTERNS WITH SPOOKY FACES.
- ADD GRAVESTONES TO THE GARDEN.
- DRAW COBWEBS, GIANT SPIDERS, OR BATS.
- GIVE THE DOORWAY SOME SCARY FANGS.

What Comes Next?

FALL IS A BEAUTIFUL SEASON IN MANY PARTS OF THE UNITED STATES. TREES TURN FIERY SHADES OF RED, ORANGE, AND GOLD. PEOPLE GO LEAF PEEPING, TRAVELING TO SEE THE BEST DISPLAYS OF FALL COLOR.

STUDY THESE FIVE ROWS OF FALL-THEMED PATTERNS. IN EACH ROW, WORK OUT WHAT PICTURE COMES NEXT, AND DRAW IT IN THE EMPTY SPACE.

HOW MANY HAY BALES?

Fall is harvest time. People celebrate the season at harvest festivals, where they can enjoy pumpkin carving, apple picking, hayrides, and getting lost in corn mazes!

This festival has a hay-bale mountain for children to climb on. Can you work out how many hay bales there are in the picture? Remember to count the bales that are hidden behind or underneath the bales you can see.

HINT:
Count the bottom layer first, then the top two layers.

ANSWER:

54

Thanksgiving Spot the Difference

Thanksgiving is celebrated every year on the fourth Thursday in November. People travel from all over the US to be with their family, watch parades, and eat a traditional Thanksgiving meal of turkey, cranberry sauce, and pumpkin pie.

There are eight differences between these two Thanksgiving pictures. Find and circle them all.

Mission to the
MOON

APOLLO 11

Between 1969 and 1972, the United States sent 24 American astronauts to the Moon. 12 of them are the only people ever to have walked on its surface.

The US space program, NASA, hopes to return astronauts to the Moon in the next few years. Your job is to design a mission patch for the historic trip. Astronauts wear mission patches on their spacesuits. Every space mission has its own patch, specially designed by its crew.

THIS IS THE
1969 MISSION
PATCH!

DRAW YOUR
PATCH HERE

WRITE A WISH

On New Year's Eve, crowds gather in Times Square, New York City, to greet the New Year. At midnight, a ball drops from the top of One Times Square, and 3,000 pounds of rainbow-colored confetti is released into the air. The confetti contains tens of thousands of notes from people around the world, with their wishes of hope, peace, and love for the New Year.

What would you wish for? Write down four wishes on the pieces of confetti below.

ANSWERS

PAGE 7: WHERE AM I?

Butter cow—Iowa
Roswell—New Mexico
Gold nuggets—California
Underwater Music Festival—Florida

PAGE 8: I-SPY 4TH OF JULY

PAGE 9: STARS & STRIPES PUZZLE

PAGE 10: STATE CAPITAL WORD SEARCH

PAGE 11: TELL A TALL TALE

- Lumberjack
- Pancakes
- Ox
- Rattlesnakes
- Hornet's nest
- Cannonball
- Bear
- Coyotes
- Cowboy
- Tornado

PAGE 12: KALEIDOSCOPE OF CULTURE

1. English
2. Spanish
3. Chinese

PAGE 14: WHAT'S WRONG ON THE TRAIL?

PAGE 15: GOLD RUSH!

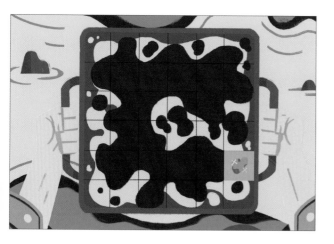

PAGE 16: RODEO RECALL

1. Brown
2. Four
3. 52
4. Red

PAGE 18: OFF TO THE FAIR

1. C) 19,200
2. B) Igloo building
3. B) 300
4. A) Food on a stick
5. C) Thomas Jefferson

PAGE 19: UP, UP, AND AWAY!

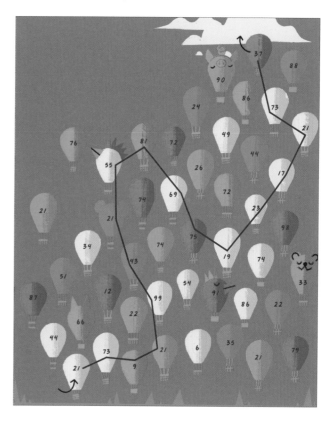

PAGE 20: THE FIRST AMERICANS

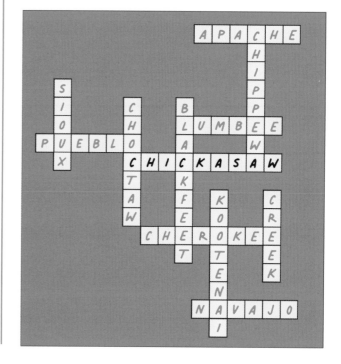

PAGE 22: SOCCER JERSEY TRIANGLE

PAGE 23: CRACK THE SUPER BOWL CODES
1. New England Patriots
2. Tom Brady
3. Pizzas

PAGE 24: BASEBALL MATCHUP

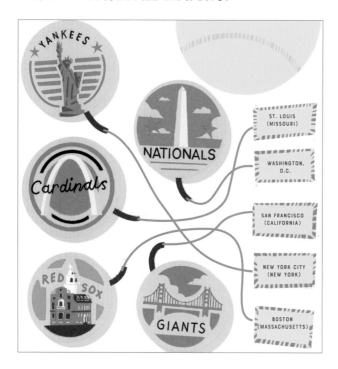

PAGE 25: BASKETBALL BRAINTEASER

PAGE 26: IT'S A GOAL!
Player A scores a goal.

PAGE 28: MOTOR RACE MATCH

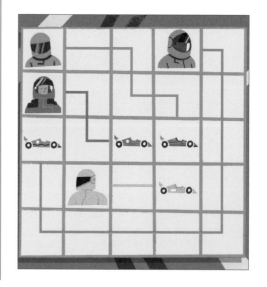

PAGE 29: PRESIDENTS CROSSWORD

PAGE 30: WHO AM I?

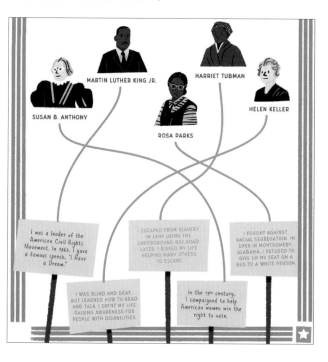

PAGE 31: JAZZ SUDOKU

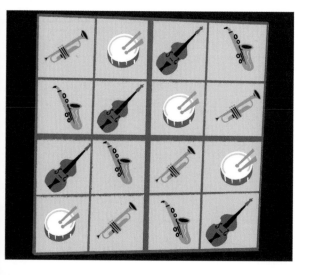

PAGE 32: MARDI GRAS MEMORY CHALLENGE

- Beads
- Doubloon/coin
- Mask
- Hat
- Balloon
- Drum
- Trumpet
- Rocket

PAGE 34: MADE IN THE USA

PAGE 35: A SLICE OF PIE

PAGE 36: WHAT'S FOR BREAKFAST?
Orange juice—$3
Stack of pancakes—$6
Blueberries—$2

PAGE 37: ON THE ROAD
The route takes you past: Carhenge;
the Fremont Troll; Cadillac Ranch;
Longaberger Company HQ;
Lucy the Elephant.

PAGE 38: WHICH STATES ON THE PLATES?

Oklahoma

Nevada

Hawaii

Rhode Island

PAGE 39: DRIVE-IN MOVIE NIGHT

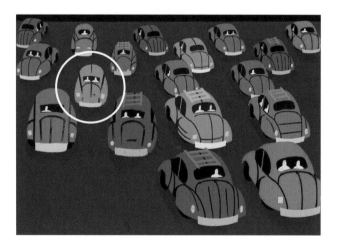

PAGE 44: WHAT A GREAT IDEA!

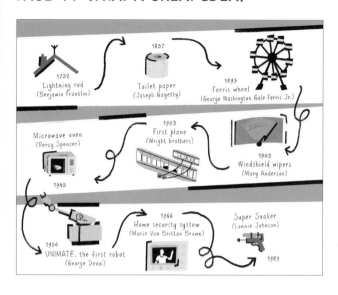

PAGE 45: THE GREAT OUTDOORS

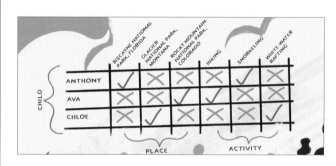

PAGE 47: STATE MOTTO CIPHER
1. Alaska
2. Montana
3. Texas

PAGE 50: BOSTON MARATHON MAZE

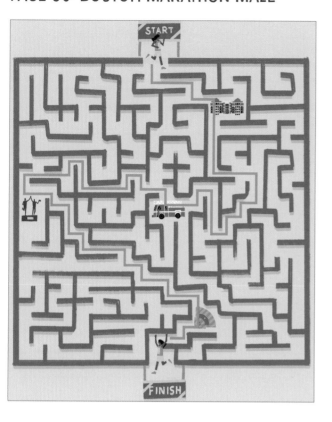

PAGE 51: WHICH FOOD, WHICH STATE?

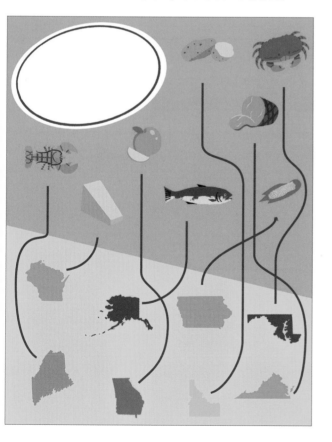

PAGE 53: WHAT COMES NEXT?

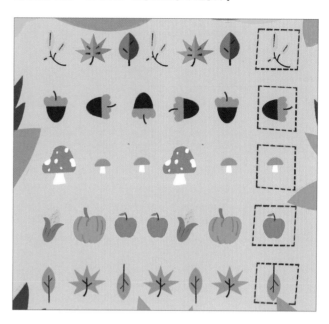

PAGE 54: HOW MANY HAY BALES?

16 (12 on the bottom, four on the top)

PAGE 55: THANKSGIVING
SPOT THE DIFFERENCE

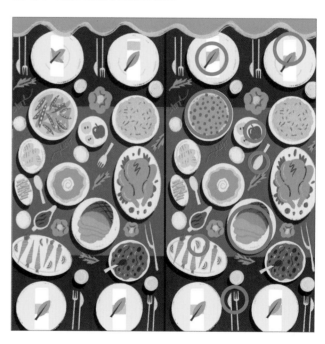

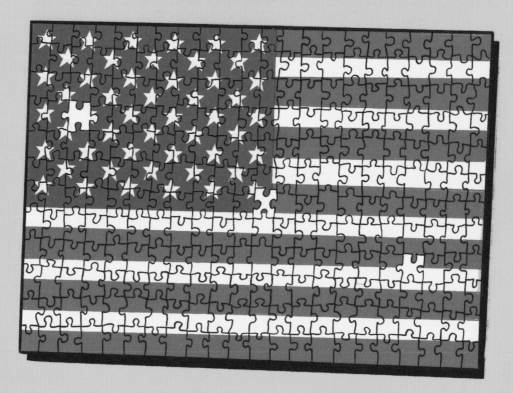

First American Edition 2022
Kane Miller, A Division of EDC Publishing

Spirit of the USA Activity Book © 2022 Quarto Publishing plc

For information contact:
Kane Miller, A Division of EDC Publishing
5402 S 122nd E Ave
Tulsa, OK 74146
www.kanemiller.com
www.myubam.com

Manufactured in Guangdong, China TT1021

ISBN: 978-1-68464-284-7

1 2 3 4 5 6 7 8 9 10